As we walk down the street,
Our hearts all aglow.

Play me some music,
With a full marching band,

A carnival of colors,
And costumes, so grand!

Play me some music,
With a quartet of strings,
A swirl of fine dancers,
Twelve swans with white wings.

Play me some music
On a guitar, extra loud!

We'll jump up and down
And join in with the crowd.

Play me some music
On a piano and drum,
A true birthday wish
With a cake, yum-yum-yum!

Play me some music
On a harp and a flute,

For ladies in ball gowns
And men in smart suits.

Play me some music
On a violin, so blue.
A goodbye message
From us, sent to you.

Play me some music
On a bright tambourine,

The finest school show
That you'll ever have seen!

Play me some music
On a black clarinet,
A soft lullaby...
My favorite one yet!

Music is everywhere!
Just listen, you'll see,

From the sounds of the city
To under the sea...

So pick up an instrument
And start to play.
Music is magic, it can brighten your day!

# Now it's your turn...

Can you play me a tune?
RAT-A-TAT-TAT! Tap a tub with a spoon!
Try shaking a treat jar, or clapping your hands...
CRASH! Play the cymbals with the lids of two pans!